MY FAVORITE GHOST

ALSO BY STEPHEN ROOS

My Horrible Secret
The Terrible Truth
My Secret Admirer
The Incredible Cat Caper *(with Kelley Roos)*
Confessions of a Wayward Preppie
The Fair-Weather Friends
Thirteenth Summer

My Favorite Ghost

by Stephen Roos

Illustrations by Dee deRosa

Troll Associates

A TROLL BOOK, published by Troll Associates,
Mahwah, NJ 07430

Published by arrangement with Macmillan Publishing Company, Inc.
For information address Macmillan Publishing Company, Inc.,
866 Third Avenue, New York, New York 10022.

First Troll Printing, 1990

Printed in the United States of America.

10 9 8 7 6 5 4 3 2 1

ISBN 0-8167-1824-5

MY FAVORITE GHOST

1

THE SUN HAD FALLEN into the Atlantic Ocean an hour before, and clouds obscured the moon and the stars. The wind was picking up too, warning that a nor'easter was on its way to Plymouth Island.

The children on the beach didn't notice. The bluff behind them protected them from the wind, and the charcoal burning at the center of their circle provided them with heat and light.

Derek Malloy was lying on his back. He propped himself on his left elbow and rested his right hand on his stomach. He was feeling too wonderfully stuffed to worry about the weather. The first week in August, Grandma Edna treated his two sisters, their friends, and him to

a real New England clambake. His grandmother spent the afternoon preparing it on the beach and left at sunset when the children and their friends arrived. All they had to do was eat, clean up, and triple check that every ember in the fire was out when they were ready to go. Some parties, she said, were better if they were kids only. It was special to be out at Horseshoe Cove instead of on the beach near Grandma's house.

As Derek patted his stomach, he counted. Under normal, everyday circumstances, Derek liked to count money, how much he had and how much he was going to have someday. At the beginning of the summer he had counted the money his sister Kit had brought with her for the summer, even though she had told him it was none of his business. Most of the summer, as assistant manager at the box office of his grandmother's summer theater, he had counted how much money the Red Barn took in each night and tried to figure out how much more it would make if Grandma Edna would raise the ticket prices.

Tonight was one of those rare occasions when Derek was counting food instead of money: one lobster plus an additional claw, which his little sister hadn't been able to finish, a dozen steamed clams swimming in butter and broth, five ears of corn, two chicken legs and three wings, a bowl of cole slaw, two helpings of strawberry shortcake. . . . Derek stopped counting. He was afraid that he might make himself sick. For once, Derek Malloy knew when enough was enough.

Even though he could barely move, the other kids were still game for more food. After the shortcake, it was time for marshmallows, and the others were roasting theirs in the fire.

His little sister, Margo, eight years old, blond and pretty, was eating the burned skin from a marshmallow at the end of a stick. His other sister, Kit, who was twelve, a year younger than Derek, was eating marshmallows directly from the plastic bag they came in. Kit was a good sister, though not as pretty or as blond as Margo. Kit had short, straight hair and a serious face. She was also given to impatience. She didn't enjoy waiting, even for her marshmallows to get black and crusty.

Mackie Vanderbeck held a marshmallow on a stick over the fire with one hand while, with his other hand, he took another marshmallow from the bag and popped it into his mouth. He was Derek's age, but he looked younger, partly because he was a little shorter and partly because he still had his baby fat. Derek knew how much Mackie wished he were thinner, but from the way Mackie was wolfing down the marshmallows, Derek figured Mackie liked the marshmallows more.

"Perfect, Pink. Just the way I like it," Phoebe Wilson said as she took a marshmallow from the end of the stick that Pink Cunningham was holding out for her. "Toasty brown," she said. "Not all black and scabby." She popped the marshmallow into her mouth and smiled sweetly, almost privately, as though Pink were the only other person sitting around the campfire. Derek couldn't figure it. The month before, Pink and Phoebe hadn't been on speaking terms. Now they were practically going together.

Derek Malloy had a list of priorities and girlfriends weren't even close to the top of it. Except for an occasional pig-out, an afternoon of sailing on Plymouth Bay, or a couple of sets of tennis with Mackie, Derek preferred to concentrate on what he considered more serious things.

"Time for ghost stories," Margo shouted as she picked some marshmallow crust from her upper lip. "Tell the one about the kid with two heads, Kit."

"But she told it last year," Derek said.

"It'll be better the second time around," Margo insisted. "I love to hear about that kid with the two heads. Imagine always having someone your own age to talk to."

"It's not a true story, you know," Derek said.

"I know that," Margo said. "If it were true, I'd be a horrible little girl for liking it so much."

"That's one way to look at it," Derek said. "But why can't we talk about something real? Like Phoebe's trip to Europe. Or the school Mackie is going to in the fall, the one Pink is applying to. Anything real is more interesting than anything that isn't."

"Says who?" Margo asked.

"Says just about anyone over eight," Derek said.

Margo scooped up two handfuls of sand. For a second, Derek thought she was about to throw them in his face. Instead she let the sand fall between her fingers. "Then someone tell a *real* ghost story," she said.

"That's a contradiction in terms," Derek said.

"What's that supposed to mean?" Margo asked.

"Since there's no such thing as real ghosts, there's no such thing as real ghost stories," Derek said.

"Ghosts aren't real?" Margo asked. "None of them?"

"Of course not," Derek said. "They're made up. You should know that by now."

"I knew some of them were fakes," Margo admitted. "But I figured there had to be some real ones somewhere."

"Well, they're all frauds," Derek said.

"You sure about that?"

"Absolutely," Derek said. "There's never been a real ghost. Not ever. I'm willing to bet on it."

"You're willing to bet on anything," Mackie said.

"Only sure things," Derek said. "Anyone want to bet there's not one real ghost in this world?" He looked from Margo to Kit to Mackie. The three of them were shaking their heads. He looked at Phoebe, who was still looking more interested in Pink than in the conversation. He looked at Pink. Pink was holding out another toasted marshmallow for Phoebe, but Pink was looking at Derek.

"You're not shaking your head," Derek said. "You ever see a real ghost, Pink?"

"I've never seen one," Pink said. "But I heard about one right here on Plymouth Island."

The flames in the campfire burned higher as the four other faces turned toward Pink.

"A local ghost?" Margo gasped. "What's his name? How old is he?"

"It's a her," Pink said. "She's very, very old and her name is Evangeline Coffin."

"And she's a real ghost?" Mackie asked.

"My dad says that when he was a kid here there were folks who swore they'd seen her."

There was a hush. Margo turned to Kit and Kit turned to Mackie and Mackie turned to Derek. Derek turned to Phoebe, who as usual was still looking at Pink.

"Was she a summer ghost or a year-rounder?" Margo asked.

"Year-round," Pink said somberly. "She was born on the island and never set foot off it. There used to be a lot of folks who stayed here till they died. Except that in Evangeline's case, she stayed on after she died. At least that's what they say."

"Evangeline," Kit murmured. "What a peculiar name."

"There used to be a number of girls by that

name," Pink said. "And of course the Coffins have been on Plymouth Island since the beginning. There are still some Coffins around."

"Above ground?" Derek asked.

Pink nodded. "And some people say that Evangeline Coffin is one of them."

"Is she a happy ghost, Pink?" Margo asked. "The one on television is happy but he's kind of a wimp."

"No. They say Evangeline is not a happy ghost at all," Pink said.

"How'd she get to be so unhappy?" Derek asked, trying not at all to hide the skepticism he felt.

"It's a grisly story," Pink said.

There was a loud, collective moan. Derek wanted to remind the kids that ghosts weren't real, but he found himself wanting to know more about Evangeline anyway.

"What did she do?" Mackie asked. Derek noticed that Mackie was so absorbed that he didn't have a marshmallow in either one of his hands.

"She murdered her husband," Pink said. "She murdered him in cold blood."

"Oh no!" Margo shrieked delightedly.

"How did she do it?" Kit asked.

"No one knows for sure," Pink said ominously. "They never found the body."

"How awful!" Phoebe cried.

"How terrifying!" Kit exclaimed.

"How stupid," Derek said. "If there was no body, how does anyone know there was a murder?"

"Evangeline's husband was a whaling captain," Pink said. "Evangeline said he never returned from his last voyage. Folks around here said she bumped him off *before* he set off on that last voyage."

"What about the other crew members?" Derek asked. "They'd have to know if their captain was aboard, wouldn't they?"

"That's the mystery that no one has been able to solve," Pink said. "A week out to sea, there was a mutiny aboard the *Infidel*. Lots of men died and all the records were destroyed. The survivors vowed never to speak about the voyage. No one was ever able to learn if the captain had been killed during the mutiny or if he was even aboard when the ship left port."

"But would the *Infidel* have left port without the captain?" Derek asked.

"It's possible," Pink said. "There was speculation that the officers set sail after the captain didn't show and the crew mutinied because the officers had taken the power into their own hands. There was also speculation that the captain was aboard and the crew cast him adrift on a raft. All anyone knows for sure is that for thirty years Evangeline stood on her widow's walk, staring out to sea. Some folks said she really, truly believed he would come back to her. Most folks believed she was putting on an act."

"Why'd she kill him?" Phoebe asked.

"The captain was in love with someone else, they said. They said Evangeline killed the captain in a fit of jealousy. When she died, she became a ghost. People haven't seen her ghost for quite a while, but they say the ghost is still there."

"Where's the house?" Derek asked.

"Across the bay," Pink said. As he raised his hand to point it out, a bolt of lightning illuminated the sea and small drops of rain began to fall. "The house has been deserted for almost a century, and it's so run-down that it won't be long before it falls into the sea."

There was more lightning. As Derek's eyes followed the tip of Pink's finger across the bay, he saw the house silhouetted by the lightning at the top of Plymouth Bluff.

"I've seen that house a thousand times," Derek said. "I didn't know there was a mystery that went with it."

"You've been spending too much time in Grandma's box office," Kit said. "I'd heard the place was haunted but that was about all I ever heard."

"Me too," Mackie said. "I thought everyone knew to stay away from the Coffin mansion."

"Didn't the police investigate?" Derek asked. "Didn't anyone ever go inside to look for the body?"

"Well, no one could do anything as long as Evangeline was still alive," Pink said. "But after she died, kids were always breaking in. They checked out the walls and the attic but they never found anything."

"How about the cellar?" Derek asked. "That would be a perfect place to bury someone you hate."

"They found a shallow hole there," Pink said. "It might have been used as a temporary grave or it might have been used for a root cellar. No one could tell for sure."

There was another roll of thunder and the raindrops grew heavier. Margo began to scream. "Let's get out of here," she cried. "Someone take me home. Please," she added desperately.

"What's wrong with her?" Mackie asked. "Evangeline get to her?"

"She's afraid of thunder and lightning," Kit explained as she hurriedly slipped on her sneakers. "She'll want to hide under a bed till the storm passes, and I'll probably want to join her."

"You're frightened of lightning?" Phoebe asked.

"Hearing about Evangeline gives me the creeps!" Kit said.

"You believe in that stuff?" Derek asked.

"Let's say I'm keeping an open mind," Kit replied.

She led Margo up the bluff to the road while Derek threw sand on the embers that the rain had not already doused. Pink and Mackie and Phoebe picked up the blankets and plastic bags and dragged them along the beach. Soon they were all biking home, with Margo sitting forlornly on Kit's handlebars.

It wasn't the way their annual clambake was supposed to end, Derek thought. But at least Margo got her scare. Even if there was no way that Evangeline could be a real ghost, Derek couldn't help thinking about her. When he arrived home, soaking wet, he was still thinking about Evangeline and wondering what it would be like if ghosts were real.

2

THE STORM THAT NIGHT was violent, and the pauses between the great flashes of lightning and drum rolls of thunder were brief. Derek dropped his wet clothes in a heap in the bathroom and slipped into his pajamas. He got onto his bed rather than into it. He lay on his stomach with his hands folded beneath his chin and watched the rain pelt the windowpanes. The storm was fierce but it didn't frighten him. Terror of the elements was Margo's department. It wasn't a Malloy family trait. When Derek felt he'd seen enough of the storm, he pulled the sheet and summer blanket over his shoulders and packed the pillow beneath his head. He was asleep before the thunder had cracked twice more.

The next morning, the sun was in Derek's eyes as soon as he opened them. He ran to the window and looked out. The waves in Plymouth Harbor were still rough from the storm, and seaweed was piled high on the beach. A branch from Grandma Edna's favorite elm lay on the lawn, and there were leaves scattered about. An hour or two of raking would remove all the evidence of the storm.

Derek pulled one end of the sheet and the summer blanket to the head of the bed, plumped up his pillow, and threw the chenille bedspread over everything. Kit said it didn't count as making his bed, but for Derek it was good enough. Why spend half his morning lining up the sheets and the blankets and making hospital corners, when he'd just have to do it again the next morning? There were other, more productive things to do with one's day, he thought. Eating breakfast and getting to his job in the box office of the Red Barn were the first two more productive things that came to mind.

He crossed the landing and started down the back stairs. Grandma's house was enormous, with staircases in the front and the back. There were so many bedrooms on the second floor that the summer before he had taken to moving to a new bedroom on the first of every month. But Derek was thirteen now, too old for that sort of kid stuff.

He heard the sizzle of the grill and smelled the French toast from the bottom of the stairs. As he turned into the kitchen, he saw that Margo and Kit and his grandmother were already sitting at the table, drinking their orange juice and eating their breakfast.

Margo sometimes said she wished that Grandma Edna looked more like other grandmothers, with white hair, spectacles, and heavy black leather shoes. Derek decided, however, that Grandma Edna looked pretty good with her black hair wrapped in a bandana, a brightly colored Indian blouse, black slacks, and sandals. She looked slightly theatrical, which was only proper and fitting since she owned and operated the Red Barn Theater next door.

"How about some French toast to get you started this morning?" Herb Kramer asked. He was standing at the stove, dipping bread into some batter. Herb was Grandma's age and he was her best friend. He was also the manager at the Red Barn's box office and Derek's boss.

Herb lived in a bungalow three blocks away, but he took his meals with Grandma Edna and most of the time he cooked them too.

"I'd like a major helping, please," Derek said as he sat down between Margo and his grandmother. "I'm ravenous."

"Coming right up," Herb said. "That storm take it out of you too?"

"Slept right through it," Derek said. "How about you guys?" He turned to Margo. The others, he knew, could live through thunder and lightning, but he wasn't so sure about his younger sister.

"It's nothing for me to be ashamed of," Margo said defensively. "Some children are more sensitive than others."

"You spend the whole night under Kit's bed?" Derek asked.

"Not the whole night," Kit said. "Around four she climbed in with me. Her snoring was worse than the thunder, as far as I'm concerned."

"Let's talk about something else," Margo said quickly.

Grandma Edna put her arm around Margo's shoulder and kissed the top of her head. "Anything you prefer to talk about, dear?"

"Don't coddle her," Derek said. "She's spoiled enough."

"I am not," Margo said vehemently. "I'm not spoiled nearly enough."

There was a knock on the door and Herb went to answer it. Mr. Hankins, the postman, handed Herb a pile of letters, which Herb placed in front of Grandma Edna.

"If they're bills, I don't want any," Grandma Edna said. "It's too nice a day for money."

Derek raised his eyebrows. He didn't see how any day could be that nice. "If you'd raise the ticket prices at the theater, you wouldn't have to worry about bills, Grandma. You'd love paying them."

Edna smiled and flipped through the mail. "That I'll never love," she said. "Here's a letter from your mother."

"It's going to say which boat they're taking next week," Margo said, suddenly looking a lot happier. It had been six weeks since the Malloy kids had left their parents back home in Grandview Heights. There wasn't much free time on Plymouth Island for Derek to miss them, but he figured it must be different for an eight-year-old kid.

"Oh, dear," Grandma Edna said as she

read the letter to herself. "They won't be here next week, after all."

"They're not coming?" Kit asked.

"They have to postpone their visit," Grandma said. "Your father's real estate business is doing so well that he can't leave it this month and that paper your mother is working on for the medical convention needs more work, she says. Neither of them can get away."

Derek saw little tears forming in Margo's eyes. "But they're coming, aren't they?" he asked. "You said they've just postponed their visit."

"To Labor Day," Grandma Edna said. "Practically the end of the summer, I'm afraid."

"I wish Daddy didn't have a business," Margo sighed. "I wish my mom wasn't a doctor. It's not fair!"

She started to cry in earnest now, and the tears streamed down her face. The sobs grew louder until Grandma Edna took Margo in her arms and held her tight. Kit moved closer to Margo and began to stroke her hair softly.

Even if Margo was spoiled rotten, the sight of her crying her eyes out made Derek feel lousy. He wished there was something he could do to cheer her up, but the things one did for an

eight-year-old girl were better done by a grandmother or an older sister.

"You were okay yesterday?" Herb asked.

Margo nodded slowly and let Grandma
Edna wipe her face with a paper napkin.

"Well, we're still here," Herb said. "So
maybe today can be as good as yesterday was.
You've got me and your grandmother and
you've got Kit and Derek too."

Margo's eyes moved from face to face.
"Even Derek?" she asked.

"As older brothers go, I'm a pretty decent
representative of the species," Derek said.

"You'd do things with me?" Margo asked.

"But you like to do things with Kit,"
Derek said. "Kit's a girl. Older sisters are for
doing things with. Not older brothers."

"Why, Derek!" Grandma said. "That's not
true."

"But there's nothing to do," Derek sighed.
"I don't want to stand in front of a mirror with
you all day and play with clothes and lipstick.
And you don't want to work with me all day in
the box office, do you, Margo?"

"I do too!" Margo said, practically shout-
ing it. "That's just exactly what I'd like to do. I
want you to teach me to play with money."

"It's not play," Derek said indignantly.

"It's fun, isn't it?"

"Yes, but . . ."

"Then let's do it," Margo said. "Big brother and little sister the way it's supposed to be."

"That'll be okay, won't it, Herb?" Grandma asked. "You can always use some extra help in the box office. And it would certainly provide Margo with a pleasant distraction."

"I'm afraid I can't help there till the end of the summer," Herb said. "I was planning to speak to Derek about the box office this morning after breakfast."

"You mean no work for Margo," Derek said. "Gee, sorry, kid."

"I mean no work for you either," Herb said hesitantly. "The play that's on is sold out. And no one's buying tickets yet for the next production."

"But there are ledgers to be balanced," Derek said. "I bet it would be a lot of fun for Margo to watch me do that."

Derek saw Margo scowl. "I want to count money," she said. "I'd like to hand out the salaries."

"I do that myself," Herb said. "And Derek's balanced all the ledgers. With costs

24

being what they are, we just can't afford to keep on someone we don't have work for."

"You mean I'm laid off?" Derek asked. "Is that what you're trying to tell me, Herb?"

"I'm sorry," Herb said. "Next show we'll have some work for you. Hang in there, Derek."

"But I've got to work," Derek said. "It's my identity. It's who I am."

"You can spend your free time finding another identity," Kit said.

"And you can find an identity for me while you're at it," Margo added.

Derek covered his face with his hands. "Yesterday I was a productive member of society. Today I'm out on my ear."

"You've got me," Margo chimed in.

"What a lovely time the two of you can have together," Grandma said.

"Please, Grandma."

"We could tell each other ghost stories," Margo said excitedly. "Now."

"I don't tell stories," Derek said. *"No one* tells stories this early in the day."

"You would if you could make money out of it," Kit volunteered.

"You willing to pay?"

Kit shook her head but she was smiling. As

far as Derek was concerned, she was enjoying his discomfort much too much.

"If I can't work at the box office for the next couple of weeks, I'm just going to have to find some other way to make money," Derek said. "If no one wants to hire me, I'll become an entrepreneur. One way or the other, I'm getting work. Sorry, Margo. It's nothing personal."

He looked at his younger sister, but he couldn't tell if she was devastated or just very unhappy that they wouldn't be hanging out together. He was about to ask her, but he decided against it. If he knew how bad she felt that he didn't want to play with her for the rest of the month, he would feel like a rat.

The trouble was that, in spite of his best efforts to convince himself otherwise, he already was feeling a little bit like one and he didn't know why on earth he was.

3

"**D**O YOU THINK I'M ROTTEN, Grandma?" he asked as he started to rinse the breakfast dishes and set them on the drainer beside the sink.

"On occasion," Grandma Edna said. She was also at the sink, filling her watering can. "We're all rotten on occasion," she continued as she doused the gloxinia in the window. "Even grandmothers."

"I'm thinking more about grandsons," Derek said. "And I'm thinking of the occasion when I skip out on my little sister."

"If you're feeling rotten, why not reconsider?" she asked cheerfully.

"Who wants to be a baby-sitter to an eight-year old?"

"Not a lot of boys your age, I suspect," Edna said. "Don't be too hard on yourself." She watered her last plant and set the can on the windowsill. "Will you make sure you dry everything?"

"All by myself?"

"I'll get you an assistant," Grandma said as she leaned toward the window. "Margo, dear. Come on in. Your brother needs you."

"If it's for the dishes, forget it," Margo called back.

"Even eight-year-olds have their responsibilities around here," Edna said. "Come help your brother."

Grandma Edna held the screen door open for Margo and handed her a dish towel. "Enjoy your little tête-à-tête, children," she said.

"You want to tell me a ghost story now?" Margo asked as she picked up the forks and started to dry them.

"How come you like ghost stories so much and you're so frightened of thunder and lightning?" Derek asked as he handed her a glass he had just rinsed.

"Well, now that I know ghosts aren't real,

it's okay to be scared by them," Margo said. "Thunder and lightning are real. That's the difference."

"I guess I never looked at it that way," Derek admitted. "What about the Widow Coffin? Didn't you think she was real?"

"Not after you explained she couldn't be," Margo said.

"But the others thought she might be real."

"I'm taking your word for it," Margo said. "So now will you tell me a ghost story?"

"I don't do ghost stories," Derek said. "I already told you that."

"Even if I pay you?" she asked. "How about a nickel?"

"I'm holding out for a dime."

Margo rested a saucer on the counter and reached into her pocket. She drew out a dime and handed it to Derek. "I'm waiting," she said.

"How do you want me to start?" he asked. "It's your dime."

"Dreams are a good way to start," she said confidently.

"Sounds okay to me. When did I have a dream?"

"Last night," Margo said. "Tell me you saw an old lady. She was so old it was scary.

She had a broom in one hand and she was chasing after you."

"Where was I running?"

"You were running you don't know where," Margo said. "But you were running from the house we saw last night. It was the widow's house. We saw it when the lightning came up."

"The Widow Coffin," Derek said. "Was she the old lady I was running from in my dream?"

Margo nodded. "You were running from the ghost of the Widow Coffin," she squealed. "You take it from there. I want my money's worth."

"But why was she running after me?"

"That's your problem," Margo said. "Maybe she wanted something. You tell me or give my money back."

"You must be the only kid I know who'd pay for a ghost story," Derek said.

"I bet I'm not," Margo said sternly. "Most kids would pay a lot more for a really good ghost story. So what did the Widow Coffin do next, Derek?"

"Don't rush me," he said. "I'll come up with something."

The truth was that Margo had come up with something. Derek couldn't say specifically what that something was, but he knew it was the beginning of whatever he would be doing till he got back his job at the Red Barn Theater. He felt the adrenaline telling him that he was on to something great now.

"Can you keep a secret, Margo?" he asked.

"Sure I can. What's the secret?"

"I don't know yet," he stammered.

"Then why are you asking?"

"It's important, that's why."

"You're talking crazy. I want to know what happened next in the dream."

"Sorry, kid," he said excitedly. "But I've got other fish to fry."

"Then I want my dime back," Margo demanded. "And I want to know the secret."

He stuck the dime back in the palm of her hand. "You'll know the secret just as soon as I make it up."

"But all I asked for was a ghost story," she sighed.

"You'll get that too," he said. "I promise you."

He handed Margo the last cup to dry and scrambled out of the kitchen and down the front hall. It was coming to him now! Evangeline Coffin! Ghosts! Kids! Money! Who cared about the Red Barn Theater when great ideas were exploding inside his head?

Thank heaven for Evangeline Coffin, he thought. And thank heaven too for a little sister. What older brothers did without them, he'd never know.

4

DEREK WALKED DOWN the front steps and let himself out the gate. The summer had been a dry one, fine for the summer people, less fine for the lawns that were now beginning to develop brown patches on them. Thanks to the storm, though, the lawns along Water Street were looking refreshed this morning and the geraniums were looking a lot less droopy than they had the day before.

Derek turned onto Commercial Street. Most of the businesses on Plymouth Island were there. So were most of the traffic jams. Even this early in the morning, the street in front of the post office and the hardware store was jammed with cars, bikes, and mopeds. Derek looked into the windows of the boutiques, which were open only during the summer. Maybe closer to Labor Day, when there were sales, he would buy himself something. If things went well, he would have enough to buy himself a whole slew of stuff, he thought happily.

He turned onto Dock Street and walked down the hill toward the harbor. At the foot of the street was a metal sign that read "Cunningham's Boatyard."

The noise was almost deafening as a dozen men sanded and scraped at boats that had been hoisted onto the dry land. Through the clouds of dust, Derek could see Pink mending a sail that had been spread out on the wharf. Derek waved. Pink didn't see him. Derek called but Pink didn't hear. Derek walked closer and tapped Pink on the shoulder.

"What are you doing here?" Pink asked.

"Is this a bad time to talk?"

"I'm working," Pink said, holding up the sail in one hand and a tube of glue in the other. "My dad pays me by the hour too."

"It's important," Derek said. "Five minutes. Ten at the most."

Pink sighed, put down the sail and the glue, and led Derek toward the pier where it was quieter. "Five minutes at the most, Derek," he said.

"You've got to tell me more about Evangeline Coffin," Derek said.

"You sure it can't wait?" Pink asked. "It was just a story."

"But a true one, you said."

"Folks around here say so. What's it to you? I thought you didn't believe in ghosts."

"Well, I don't," Derek said, not sure he should admit that now. "Can't a fellow be interested in the occult?"

"Occult?" Pink asked.

"It means hidden things," Derek said. "Things you can't explain. Like ghosts and poltergeists."

"You going into the occult business?" Pink asked.

"How do you figure that?"

"You usually have an angle," Pink said.

"I'm flattered, of course," Derek said, and meant it. "Does everyone think I'm always out for a buck?"

"Well, aren't you?"

Derek shrugged. Could he help it if something was always more interesting to him if money was involved? "Maybe you could tell me a little more about Evangeline," he said. "Are you sure there's no grave for the captain? Did anyone ever check the cemetery?"

"The root cellar in the basement of the Coffin mansion is the closest the captain may ever have got to a regular grave," Pink said. "No one has ever found another grave of any kind. I've got to get back to work now, Derek."

Derek couldn't let Pink go just yet. He had to try out something on Pink, even though he knew it could be a terrible risk. "I had a dream last night," he said slowly. "I want to tell you about it."

Pink looked at his wristwatch. "Some other time, Derek."

"One more minute of your time is all I ask," Derek said. He put his index finger to his chin. Should he tell Pink the dream Margo had made up for him, the one about Evangeline chasing him from the house? It wouldn't be enough, Derek knew. He would have to add something. "It was scary, Pink," he said.

"If you're going to tell me, make it quick," Pink said.

"I was in a very cold place," Derek said. "Cold and damp and very, very dark."

"Like a cellar?"

"Well, I don't know. Maybe. But what I saw was really terrifying."

"Tell me, Derek."

"I saw a cross," Derek said. "It had the captain's name on it. It was awful, Pink. Really awful."

"You've got a very suggestible mind," Pink said.

"I hope you're right," Derek said as dubiously as he could. "What do you make of that, Pink?"

Pink shook his head. "Nothing, I guess," he said. "It was just a dream, wasn't it? And it's not like you believe in ghosts. So there's nothing to make of it. Right?"

"If that's what you say, that's what I'll think," Derek said. "You've been very reassuring, Pink."

The two boys started walking back to the boatyard. Derek spotted two strips of wood lying on the ground beside a Boston whaler. "Is that stuff scrap?" he asked.

"I guess so," Pink said.

"Can I have them?"

"What for?"

"You never know when something will come in handy, maybe at the theater even," Derek said.

"They're yours."

Derek picked up the pieces of wood with

one hand and waved to Pink with the other. "Thanks for listening," he said, and started to leave the boatyard. With some nails and some paint, he could turn the scraps of wood into a cross, just like the one that he had imagined over Captain Coffin's grave.

The beginning of the plan had come to him while he had been talking to Margo, and the middle had appeared while he had been talking to Pink. So far it had been easy. From now on, it would be work. For Derek, however, it was the kind of work that he loved best.

5

THE BEST WAY to work out a plan was to start a list. As far as Derek was concerned, the only thing more satisfying than starting a list was crossing off the items on it. That morning in his bedroom, Derek set out a yellow legal pad on the top of his bureau. He picked up his red felt-tipped pen and wrote: "Two pieces scrap wood."

He smiled and picked up his blue felt-tipped pen and drew a line through the words. He was on his way.

Derek picked up his red pen again and thought a moment, A small, battery-operated reading lamp would come in handy, he decided. He wrote that down too. He had seen one for sale in the Island Bookshop. It would be perfect for his purposes. He reached into the top drawer of the bureau and pulled out two ten-dollar bills that lay between his socks and his underwear.

He stuck the legal pad in the bureau for safekeeping and ran down the stairs to the kitchen. No one was there, not even Margo. Derek was glad of that. He didn't want her tagging along yet.

He grabbed an apple from the fruit bowl on the lazy Susan and let himself out the front door. He turned left on Water Street, retracing the path he had followed earlier that day. When he got to Commercial Street, the traffic was lighter than it had been earlier. It was beach weather, and anyone who could was spending the day sailing or swimming or sunbathing.

As he pushed on the door to the Island Bookshop, he heard the little bell ring above his head. Mrs. Williamson, the owner, gave him a nod before going back to another customer in the gardening section.

The shop was almost empty. The coast was all but clear. The less time he spent in the book-store, the less chance there was for someone to catch him buying the lamp.

He raised his arm and made a half wave at Mrs. Williamson. She smiled and went back to her customer. Derek would have to wait. He wished there was something to do in a bookstore. He looked at the signs above the shelves. Fiction. History. Gardening. Photography. None of them sounded promising. He saw a sign at the back of the store. "Occult." That did sound promising.

The year before, Derek had bought a book called *How to Make a Zillion Dollars in Real Estate in the Next Twenty Minutes While Watching Television.* When he finished it, he didn't see how anyone, except the author, could ever make a dime out of it. Derek hadn't bought a book since, and he hadn't borrowed one from the library either.

He walked to the occult section, however, and pulled out a book that looked different from the rest. It was hardback and it was clearly old. *Widows and Witches of the Northeastern United States* was the title. Derek thumbed through the book till he came to the index. He looked under the C's. There she was: "Coffin, Evangeline, the Witch of Plymouth Island, page 328." Derek let a small gasp rise from his chest to his mouth. Evangeline was more than a ghost. She was a bona fide witch!

"Derek Malloy in a bookstore?"

He turned suddenly. Phoebe Wilson and

Mackie Vanderbeck were standing behind him, and they looked as surprised to see him as he was to see them. He closed the book and tried to stick it back on the shelf, feeling very much as though they had caught him doing something he shouldn't have been doing in the first place.

"Hi, guys," he said as amiably as he could. "What are you up to?"

"Mackie's helping me pick out something for Pink," Phoebe said.

"It's his birthday?"

"His birthday was months ago," Phoebe said. "It's a present present."

"For no occasion at all?" Derek asked. He couldn't imagine giving anyone something for no reason at all.

"It's a semioccasion," Mackie said. "He's going for an interview at my school in a couple of weeks."

"That's it?" Derek asked.

"Well, if he gets in, he might go," Phoebe said. "And if he goes, it's a big deal. I want to get him something for that. And since Mackie's going to the school in September, he's the perfect person to help me choose."

"I never was perfect before," Mackie said. "Thanks, Phoebe. And I never saw you in a bookstore before, Derek. What gives?"

"Just browsing," Derek lied.

"In the occult section?" Phoebe asked. "I'd expect to find you in the financial section."

"I got lost," Derek said.

"What's that you've got in your hands?" Mackie asked.

"Huh?" Derek asked. He looked down and was surprised to see that he was still holding *Widows and Witches of the Northeastern United States.* For a moment, he panicked. Of all people, Phoebe and Mackie were two who weren't supposed to know what he was up to, even though he himself wasn't sure yet what his final plan was. Derek thought again. Maybe this was one of those times when he could turn the moment to his advantage. He held up the book for Mackie and Phoebe to read. He didn't know whether to be irritated or pleased when they both laughed out loud.

"You're turning into a believer?" Phoebe asked.

"I'm interested is all," Derek said, slightly defensively.

"But last night you said there was no such thing as a real ghost," Mackie said. "Have you changed your mind?"

"Something happened," Derek said as slowly and as meaningfully as he could. "I had a dream. A terrifying dream about Evange-line."

"What happened in the dream?" Phoebe asked.

"I don't think I can talk about it," Derek said. "It was too scary. She was after me is all I can say."

"So you think she's for real now?" Mackie asked.

"I'm just taking ghosts a lot more seriously today," Derek said. "Let's leave it at that."

"I know you, Derek Malloy," Phoebe said. "You're up to something."

"Are these bags under my eyes just pre-tend?" Derek asked. "Do you think I got them from sleeping soundly last night?"

"I don't see any bags," Phoebe said suspi-ciously.

"Look closer."

"Maybe," she said. "Maybe you've always had little bags under your eyes."

"Thanks for the vote of confidence," Derek said.

"Do you think Derek would be spending his hard-earned money on a book about witches if he weren't serious about them?" Mackie asked.

"You've got a point there," Phoebe said. "How much does that book cost?"

Derek anxiously flipped open the cover. On the flyleaf was the price: nine dollars. He'd had no intention of buying the book. Now he had no choice in the matter. He had trapped himself. "It's a steal at twice the price," he said.

"Well, I'm convinced your dream was for real even if witches and ghosts aren't," Mackie said. "I'm sorry I was suspicious, Derek."

"Well, I'm not," Phoebe said. "With Derek, there's bound to be a trick."

"You hurt me, Phoebe," Derek said. "More than I can ever say."

Mrs. Williamson had returned to her cash register and not a moment too soon. Derek tucked the book under his arm and walked away. Phoebe was going to prove a tough customer, but he'd get to her sooner or later. Her suspicion was going to be a challenge, not a problem.

"Will that be it, Derek?" Mrs. Williamson asked.

"I'd like that too," Derek said as he pointed to the lamp on the counter.

"That comes to nineteen ninety-five," she said as she took the two ten-dollar bills from him.

Derek's capital investment in his project was almost twice what he had anticipated. But for once he didn't mind. Thinking big shouldn't be a problem for an entrepreneur. From here on in, he would just have to think bigger.

When he got home, he could add the book to his list and then cross it *and* the lamp off. While he was at it, he would add his last item: an assistant, preferably a short female one.

6

WHEN HE GOT BACK to the house, Margo and Grandma Edna were in the kitchen wrapping pieces of chicken in foil and pouring lemonade in thermoses.

"We're going down to the beach," Grandma Edna said. "Would you like to join us for a picnic?"

"I guess so," Derek said.

"You don't have to if you don't want to," his grandmother said almost apologetically.

"I want to," Derek assured her. He loved her picnics, and, after walking all over town that morning, he was hungry enough for one. But he didn't want anyone to see what was tucked in his shopping bag. Nor did he want them to see the Island Bookshop logo on the side of the bag. "I've got to go to my room first," he said. "For my bathing suit."

When he got upstairs, he dumped the contents of the bag onto his bed. He crumpled the bag up and threw it in the wastebasket, then examined the lamp and installed the little batteries that came with it. It worked perfectly. He switched it off and tucked it in the bottom drawer of his bureau, where no one would ever think to look.

He sat on the edge of his bed and looked up Evangeline in the index of *Widows and Witches of the Northeastern United States*. He turned to page 328:

Evangeline Coffin.

Before Derek could start reading, he heard his grandmother calling him from downstairs.

"I'll be there in a minute," he called back.

"We're leaving now, Derek, dear. You have to carry the basket."

He couldn't let his grandmother wait. He slid the book under the bed and ran downstairs. Margo was holding a thermos under each arm. The picnic basket was waiting for him on the kitchen table.

"Your suit," Margo said. "Where is it?"

"Huh?"

"You went upstairs to change, didn't you?"

"I'll be right back," he said. "Don't leave without me."

He ran back upstairs to his room, tore off his clothes, and pulled a bathing suit from his underwear drawer. After putting it on, he checked the room as he left. The tip of the book was showing underneath his bed, and he kicked it in farther. Then he ran downstairs.

"How come you forgot to change the first time?" Margo asked.

"I was distracted," he said as he picked up the basket.

"By what you had in the shopping bag?"

"What shopping bag?"

"The shopping bag you were carrying, silly," Margo said. "The one from the bookstore."

"You said you could keep a secret," Derek said.

"It's a secret?" she asked. Her eyes widened, and the brows above them rose an inch. "That's the secret you were going to make up?"

He put an index finger to his lips to shush her and grabbed the wicker basket. Although the kid had too big a mouth, he had to admit she was observant.

His grandmother held the door for them, and they started across the lawn and down the hill to the beach behind the house.

"How come Kit's not here?" he asked.

"She and Phoebe have a tennis date," Grandma Edna said. "They'll grab a bite to eat at Phoebe's after their game." Grandma stuck the umbrella into the sand about twenty feet from the water and spread the blanket. Her beach was a private one, but she let anyone use it. Usually, there were a couple of actors from the theater there and some apprentices. This afternoon, however, the beach was empty. Derek was pleased. When there were other people around, Grandma shared whatever she brought, even the barbecued chicken. As far as Derek was concerned, there was never enough to go around.

"Thanks for the feed," he said as he opened the basket and popped some cherries into his mouth. They were for later, but they looked too ripe to wait another minute.

"Grandma made the picnic to cheer me up," Margo said. "On account of Mom and Dad not coming and me not having anyone to do things with. She feels sorry for me."

Their grandmother set out her beach chair under the umbrella and sat down so that only her legs got the sun. "I don't feel sorry for you at all," she said as she adjusted her sunglasses. "I fixed a picnic lunch because I enjoy picnics with you. Isn't that a good enough reason?"

"Are you sure you don't feel a little sorry for me, Grandma?"

"Not even the littlest bit, dear," Grandma Edna said. "Could you pour me some lemonade, please?"

Margo looked disappointed but she unscrewed the top of the thermos. She poured the lemonade into the top and let only a few drops fall on the blanket.

"Then I guess I won't feel sorry for me either," she said cheerfully. "Are you feeling sorry about being unemployed, Derek?"

Derek was chewing on a chicken leg. Before he swallowed, he took another bite. It was a stalling action. He hadn't meant to say anything about his scheme in front of his grandmother, but now he had to provide some kind of cover for all the comings and goings that were sure to fill the days ahead. "I've had a feeling that my luck is about to change," he admitted.

"How lovely!" Grandma Edna exclaimed. "You must be the most resilient grandson a grandmother ever had. Tell Margo and me all about the turnabout in your luck, dear."

"Well, it's nothing like a real job, Grandma," he said cautiously. "It's more like a project to tide me over till I get back on my feet."

"Is my luck about to change too?" Margo asked. "Am I going to get some money?"

"What do you need money for?" Derek asked. "You're only eight." Although he had plans for her, he hadn't considered sharing his profits with her.

"Eight-year-olds have needs," she said.

"If you work for Derek, make sure you get the money in advance," their grandmother said.

"Okay, I'll pay you," Derek said. The words were out of his mouth before he knew he had said them.

"You've got work for Margo?" Grandma asked. "Really, Derek?"

"Me work?" Margo asked indignantly. "I don't want to work. I just want a salary."

"Maybe Derek can give you a job doing something simple like standing and waving your arms a little."

"Okay," Margo said. "If I get the money in advance."

"Tell us about the work you've got for yourself and Margo," Grandma Edna said. She was serious now. Derek could tell because she had taken off her sunglasses and was leaning toward him. "What's up?"

Derek poured himself some lemonade and thought. It wouldn't look good if anyone, Margo included, thought she was getting a job just for the asking. "If you work for me," he said, "there are three rules you would have to follow. One is show up for work on time, even when the sun's out and you'd rather be at the beach. The second rule is always do what the boss tells you, and the third is keep your mouth shut. You think you're up to it?"

"Not the first two parts," Margo said. "Does that mean I don't get the job?"

"I'm afraid so, kid," he said, trying not to worry how he was ever going to find someone else who could fill her shoes.

"But I can keep a secret, I bet," she said.

"How can I know that for sure?"

"Well, if I get the job, I wouldn't tell anyone about that shopping bag from the bookstore you snuck into the house," she said. "And I wouldn't tell anyone about the lamp in the bag. If I don't get the job, I'd probably blab about it all over town."

"What shopping bag?" Grandma Edna asked. "What lamp?"

"It's nothing to worry about," Derek said. "I've decided to give Margo the job after all."

"What a lovely older brother you are!" Grandma Edna said. "And only this morning you didn't think you'd have time for a younger sister. Now will you tell us what on earth your project is, Derek?"

"It's too early to tell," he lied. "It needs a lot of work."

"Really?" Grandma asked. "I can hear the wheels inside your head spinning away."

Derek tried to look as noncommittal as possible, but the wheels Grandma had mentioned were spinning so fast he was almost dizzy. His plan was complete down to the last detail. He had Grandma to thank for that, he decided, as he pictured Margo waving her little arms in the air and making him rich.

All systems were go. Within hours, he would be taking the first thrilling step toward becoming an entrepreneur.

7

THAT NIGHT, before he went to bed, Derek sank to his knees and reached under the bed. It wasn't there! Derek tried hard not to panic. He raised the bedspread and looked again. In his haste that afternoon, he had slid the book farther than he had intended, too far for anyone but a basketball player to reach.

He pulled the bed from the wall and grabbed the book. He was supposed to clean his room once a week, but he rarely bothered. So he had only himself to blame for the dustballs and lint that were now attached to *Widows and Witches of the Northeastern United States.*

He remembered page 328, so he skipped the index and went straight to the reference to Evangeline. Though there were a lot of other witches along the New England coast, Evangeline certainly held her own in the ghost department. For years people from all over New England had come to Plymouth in hopes of seeing her ghost standing on the widow's walk staring out to sea. Once or twice a year her ghost had been spotted. As more and more folks saw her, she became a celebrated landmark ghost, said to walk her widow's walk for her sins. Even though no one claimed to have seen her in the last twenty years, she was still considered a prominent New England ghost.

Derek closed the book and slipped it back under his bed. He pulled the yellow legal pad from his top drawer and crossed off the reading lamp. Then he added *Widows and Witches* and crossed that off too. He couldn't have been more delighted with his progress.

He looked at the clock on his dresser. It was late, almost eleven-thirty. The last cars had pulled away from the Red Barn's parking lot more than an hour before. Herb had gone on home and Grandma had turned in for the night. Everything was still, except for the waves in the harbor and the wind rustling through the trees.

Derek couldn't wait to take his next step. This afternoon after their picnic was finished, he had decided to go out and take a look around the widow's house, and while there he had all but heard a voice cry out, "Now is the time, Derek. Go for it!" For a moment he wondered if it could be *her* voice. He had tensed and even looked toward the widow's walk before he could remind himself that there were no such things as ghosts. The voice must have been the little one in his head, the one that always told him to go ahead and do whatever he wanted. Derek had always felt blessed that he didn't have one of those "you'd better watch it, kid" voices that other people complained about.

Now it was definitely time for his next move. Derek slipped out of his bedroom and tiptoed down the hall to the bathroom. He let the water run until it was neither hot nor cold. With both hands he splashed water on his hair and his face and neck and the front of his pajamas. Still wet, he tiptoed down the hall until he was standing in front of Kit's door.

"Kit," he whispered. He knocked gently on the door because he didn't want to wake up anyone but Kit tonight.

There was no answer.

He whispered more loudly and knocked less gently.

Still no answer. Although Kit had warned him several hundred times never to enter her room unless and until she said it was okay, he opened the door and walked toward her bed.

"Kit," he whispered again. "Wake up! Help me!"

He heard Kit turn in her sleep. Then she was sitting up in bed and turning on her lamp on the bed table at the same time.

"Margo?" she groaned as she wiped the sleep from her eyes.

"It's Derek. You've got to help me."

When she opened her eyes and looked at him, she looked every bit as startled as he had hoped she would. "I thought you were Margo," Kit whispered back. "She's the one who's always sneaking in here. What are you doing here?"

"I'm scared," Derek said. "Really scared." He sat at the foot of Kit's bed. "Can I talk to you, Kit? Will you listen, please?"

"I've never seen you so upset," Kit said. "You're never afraid of anything. How come you're all wet?"

"It's sweat, Kit."

"You've been out jogging at this time of night?"

"It's a cold sweat, Kit. The kind you get with the heebie-jeebies."

"You had a nightmare? Is that it?"

"Maybe you'll say it was a nightmare, but to me it was real," Derek said. "As real as the end of your nose."

"Tell me," Kit said. "That'll help."

Derek looked at the ceiling and sighed deeply. "You remember how I made fun of Evangeline Coffin when we were at the clambake? Remember how I said there was no such thing as ghosts?"

"Even though the rest of us kind of half-believed they are for real," Kit said. "I remember."

"Tonight I dreamed about Evangeline. I dreamed I was wandering around outside her house. Kit, you'll never believe it. I saw a lamp burning on the second floor. I saw the light, Kit!"

"You really saw it?" Kit whispered. "In the dream?"

"It was a vision, Kit," Derek whispered

back. "Evangeline wants me for something. I know that light is burning in that window this very minute. It's a sign that's meant just for me, Kit."

"It can't be," Kit said. "No one ever goes near that house anymore. There's no way there could be a light there."

"It's there now," Derek said as excitedly as he could. "I could swear it's there. But there's only one way to find out," he added, hoping that he was planting a seed in Kit's mind.

"There's no way either one of us is going to find out," she said. "Go drink some warm milk. It'll help you get back to sleep."

"I'll never sleep again," Derek said. "She's haunting me. Isn't there anything you can do to help me?"

"Nothing doing. I'm afraid of ghosts."

"What if I lose my mind?"

"You're being melodramatic."

"Help me," Derek whispered. "Please, Kit. Come with me."

Kit sighed. It gave Derek hope. She threw off the covers. Derek's hopes began to soar. "Why me?" she asked. "I'll be terrified out there at night."

"I have no one else to turn to," Derek said as pathetically as he could.

"Get dressed, Derek. Quickly. Before I lose my nerve. I may be crazy but I guess we'll have to bike over to the Coffin mansion before either of us ever gets back to sleep."

"I guess I never appreciated how much you really care for me, Kit," he said.

"Get dressed, Derek."

While he was pulling on his shirt and struggling with his sweater, Derek tried not to think how touched he was by Kit's concern. Getting sentimental was a bad business practice. It could even make him feel guilty about manipulating her into doing something she was so afraid of.

He heard Kit leave her room and tiptoe down the back stairs. He followed, groping through the kitchen without turning on the light, and closing the kitchen door gently behind him.

After he had returned from the Coffin mansion that afternoon, he had left his bike by the barn door so that it would be easier to find in the night. He heard Kit fumbling around, trying to find her own bike. If he had given his plan more thought, he would have left her bike at the entrance too.

It was better, he decided, to let Kit lead the way. They walked their bikes across the lawn and down the driveway. When they got to the street, they pedaled off.

The little lights on their handlebars didn't do much good in pointing the way across the island. But the three-quarter moon let them know where they were and where they were heading. They sped down Water Street and out Dune Road. As they passed the Whalers' Church, the clock in the steeple struck midnight.

The houses on Dune Road were fewer and farther between. Now and then, Derek saw a porch light, but there was no indication of people. There was no traffic either. The only noise he heard was the wind in the pine trees. It was the same safe and quiet Plymouth Island as always, but tonight Derek shivered. If he believed in ghosts, he would have thought the shiver a sign of fear. But he didn't believe that, not for a second. It was only the cool night air that made him feel a chill.

Even so, he drew his bike closer to Kit's. They were half a mile from the Coffin mansion, and Derek thought he could see the angle of the roof and part of the widow's walk in the moonlight. Kit slowed a bit. Perhaps she had spotted the house too. Maybe she was feeling a little more frightened now.

A few moments later Kit pulled to a stop in front of the picket fence surrounding the house. Even in the moonlight it looked as though it had never been painted. They didn't have to look for a gate. Half the fence lay on the ground. Kit stepped over it and walked toward the house. Derek followed. There was no path and no lawn. Wild grass as high as their waists grew in the sandy soil.

"No light, Derek," she whispered. "Look!"

He did as Kit told him. The house seemed larger and more decrepit in the dark than it did in the daylight. It was three stories high and enormous. Shingles were falling off and many of the windows were out of their frames. There wasn't a pane that hadn't been broken.

"In the vision, the light was coming from a window on the sea side," Derek whispered.

"It was a dream. It wasn't a vision," Kit said, but her voice didn't sound so sure.

Now it was Derek's turn to lead. He stepped through the grass and walked around the side of the house. As they approached the bluff, the roar of the waves was louder and the wind stiffer. Derek saw Kit wrap her arms around her body as though she were hugging herself. She was as cold as he was.

When they reached the bluff, they turned. Derek's eye went immediately to the center window on the second floor. He had to wait a moment for Kit's eye to catch up with his. When he heard her gasp, he knew she'd seen it too.

"It's got to be the moonlight," she said anxiously. "It's got to be a reflection in the windowpane."

"But there's no glass in any of the windows," he said. "It's got to be the light. It's exactly as it was in the vision. Evangeline Coffin has turned on a light. She's calling for me, Kit. She wants me. It's the light I told you about," he said.

"It's not real," she said, her voice quaking. "There's got to be an explanation. It's nothing to be afraid of."

Could Kit really be so hard-nosed? If she wasn't impressed, his whole plan would be wrecked. But Derek didn't have to worry. As he turned from the window, he saw Kit running madly around the side of the house. He ran after her, and as he reached the picket fence, she was getting on her bike and speeding back down Dune Road.

Derek got on his own bike. "Wait for me, Kit!" he shouted. "Don't leave me here alone! I'm too frightened!"

"Me too!" she shouted back.

It had worked. Kit was every bit as frightened as he had hoped. The little battery-run reading lamp had been a very wise investment, after all. Maybe Derek would give it to her for Christmas. Tonight she had earned it.

8

KIT WAS STILL SHAKING when they got home. Derek warmed some milk and pretended it was as calming for him as it was for her. They talked for almost an hour before they went to bed. Even though Kit couldn't deny the light was real, she still couldn't believe that the ghost of Evangeline Coffin was working on Derek. Even if there was a ghost, why would she choose Derek to haunt? Derek hoped her doubts wouldn't cause trouble, but in any case, the next move was Kit's. Although Derek had spent some time, some effort, and $19.95 in setting her up for that move, she would have to believe she was making it all on her own. If she even suspected Derek's manipulation, the whole thing would blow up in his face. It was a tricky business, counting on other people to do what you wanted them to do without their knowing you wanted them to do it, but there was no way around it.

"SLEEP OKAY?" his grandmother asked as he sat down to breakfast the next morning.

"Like a log," he said. He looked across the table at Kit and gave her a halfhearted shrug. If she thought he was being brave, so much the better. "Where are Herb and Margo?" he asked.

"Berry picking," Kit said. "If there's any justice in this world, we'll be eating blueberry pancakes tomorrow morning."

"Have some cornflakes, Derek," Grandma Edna said. "This morning there's no justice or pancakes."

"I didn't mean to complain," Kit said. "I guess I didn't get enough sleep. Do you remember Mackie's telephone number, Derek?"

"Seven-eight-three-one," Derek said. "Why are you calling him?"

"Top secret," she said. "But only momentarily."

"Where are you calling him from?" he asked, hoping he didn't sound too interested.

"The sitting room off the front hall," she said. "And don't listen in on the other line. I can hear the click, Derek."

"I promise not to," Derek said. "You're at an age when it's okay to have your own little secrets."

"You're only a year older than I am," Kit said.

"And I've been there."

Kit stood and walked down the hall. Derek finished his cornflakes as quickly as possible and drained the orange juice from his glass. He took his bowl and his glass to the sink and rinsed them. He left the bowl in the sink but he held onto the glass. He walked as idly as he could down the hall.

The door to the little sitting room was closed. He put the hollow end of the glass to the door and put his ear to the other end.

"Thanks, Mackie," he heard Kit saying. "Be here at three this afternoon. Maybe we can think up a way to help Derek then."

He smiled as he heard her put down the phone. He stepped back from the door and turned toward the kitchen in case she was about to leave the sitting room. He hoped that Mackie Vanderbeck was only one of the people she was calling that morning. When the door didn't open, he applied his glass to it once again.

"Phoebe," he overheard her say. "It's Kit. Something weird is going on over here. It's Derek and Evangeline. He thinks she's for real. He's definitely spooked. And there's something else, something I can't tell you about on the phone that kind of spooks me too. Can you get over here this afternoon? Can you ask Pink to come too?"

Derek slipped the glass into his pocket and slipped himself back to the kitchen. He was grinning. Of all the sisters in the world, Kit had to be the greatest. He knew that deep down inside, she'd be concerned about him. Now she had done exactly what he wanted her to do—and he hadn't even had to ask.

HE SAT IN HIS ROOM the rest of the morning, reading and rereading the passages about Evangeline in *Widows and Witches of the Northeastern United States.* When he heard his grandmother and Margo talking out in the hall, he didn't bother to slip the book under his bed. If they found him reading it, it would be just fine for him now.

When the clock in the steeple of the Whalers' Church struck one, Derek went downstairs to fix himself a sandwich. Kit turned up at the same time to do the same thing. Derek said he was taking his sandwich upstairs to his room.

"Not feeling so hot?" she asked.

"Not bad," he said. "Strange is more like it."

Kit smiled sympathetically. "Evangeline on your mind again?"

Derek nodded sadly. "It was the vision, Kit. Just as I said. What can I do but believe it? You saw the light, didn't you?"

"There could be a reasonable explanation for it," she said.

"I wish you'd tell me."

"I don't know offhand," she replied helplessly.

"I've had another vision, Kit," he said slowly, as slowly as he could.

"Spare me," Kit said.

"Evangeline came to me again," he said. "Last night, after we got home from the Coffin mansion."

"I don't want to listen," Kit said. "You should go back to your room. Take a nap. On second thought, go to your room and *don't* take a nap. You'll probably have another one of your visions."

Derek shrugged and stuffed half of the tunafish sandwich into his mouth to keep from smiling. He put the other half of the sandwich on a plate and walked up the back stairs.

He lay down on his bed and looked out the window. It was another perfect August day. The sky was cloudless and there was a comfortable breeze. It was a day for swimming or sailing, but not as far as Derek was concerned. Today he was far better off in the sack. He reached for *Widows and Witches,* but before his hand touched it, he was drifting off to sleep. Even Derek needed to catch up on his sleep once in a while.

When he woke up, it wasn't because he had had another vision. It was something he had heard: the screen door in the back of the house slamming and low voices in the kitchen rising to his room. He got out of bed, walked to the hall, and listened from the top of the stairs.

"He's terrified, really terrified," he heard Kit saying. "He had this thing he calls a vision. The middle of the night, we were biking over to the Coffin mansion. Can you believe it?"

Derek took one step down the stairs to hear better.

"What was going on over there?" he heard Mackie say.

"Oh, nothing, not really," Kit said. "Derek said he'd had this vision in his sleep. It was something about a light in a second-floor window of the widow's house. I went with him to check it out. I was scared but I had no choice."

"In the middle of the night?" Phoebe asked.

"It was the only way to find out if his vision was for real, and he seemed so upset. After all, he is my brother, what could I do?" Kit replied.

"When there was no light, didn't he realize it was just a dream? The other day at the boatyard he told me about another bad dream he'd had," Pink said.

"That's the troubling part," Kit said. "That's why I wanted you guys over here this afternoon. When Derek and I got to the widow's house, there *was* a light in the second-floor window, just the way he'd seen it in his vision. And this morning he said he'd had another vision after we got home."

There was silence, nothing but silence. Derek wished someone would drop a pin so that he could hear. He hoped the pause would last a while too. Long pauses were more meaningful than short ones.

"You saw the light?" Pink asked. "Really saw it?"

"Well, yes," Kit said hesitantly. "Now, I

like a ghost story as much as anybody, but I'm still not a believer."

"There's an explanation," Mackie said. "A rational one. You sure it's not one of Derek's tricks?"

"What the trick is beats me. And he really does seem shaken up. That's not like Derek," Kit said. "Any ideas, Phoebe?"

"Now that you mention it, he looked awfully different when we ran into him at the bookstore," Phoebe said. "Serious, but then Derek is always serious. I guess worried is the word I'm looking for. I've never seen him look so worried before. Let's face it. No matter what *we* think, Derek does seem to think these visions are real."

"But what are we going to do?" Kit asked. "There's got to be something we can do for him."

Derek knew his cue when he heard it. He started down the stairs. He didn't want the other kids to go any further without his guidance.

"What's going on in here?" he asked as soon as he hit the landing. "What are you guys doing here?"

"Kit called us here for a powwow," Mackie said.

"And she didn't invite me?" he asked. "That hurts, Kit."

"It's all about you," Pink said. "Kit's worried. And frankly, so am I."

"Same goes for me," Mackie said.

"Me too," Phoebe added.

"What's it all about, Kit?" Derek asked. "Why would anyone ever be worried about me? What could be wrong?"

"It's your visions," Kit said. "I decided it was time to go for outside help. I can't do it alone."

"You need to find out what's at the bottom of your visions," Mackie said. "Maybe we can help."

"We're your friends, Derek," Pink said.

"It's a time when you need your friends," Phoebe said. "Don't be too proud to ask for help."

"Thanks, guys," Derek said. "But I don't know how anyone can help me. Maybe my visions are just nightmares, like Kit says. Or maybe I'm just losing my ever-loving mind. It's my problem and I have to take care of it on my own. Of course, there was the light in the window. . . ."

"Kit says she saw that too," Mackie said.

"Maybe we were both hallucinating," Derek

said. "Insanity is supposed to run in families, I hear."

"I saw it, Derek," Kit protested. "And it's not the power of suggestion. In the twelve years we've lived under the same roof, I have never taken one suggestion from you."

"But she doesn't believe in Evangeline," Phoebe said.

"She's probably right," Derek said. "You guys shouldn't worry about me or Evangeline. The ghost and I will go it alone." He took a step back up the stairs. Then he looked back. The four of them were still sitting at the kitchen table, and they were staring hard at him. "I mean it, guys. I don't want you to get involved with my problems."

"Maybe Derek's right," Pink said. "Sometimes problems are best solved if you leave them alone. How about the four of us going for a sail? You too, Derek, if you're interested."

As he stood at the bottom of the steps with his right hand on the railing, he panicked. Had he gone too far to convince them that he had any intention of taking care of Evangeline on his own?

"I'm too exhausted to go sailing," he moaned.

"Then take a nap?" Phoebe suggested.

"I'll probably have another vision if I take another nap," he said. "If it's any worse than the latest one, I could quite conceivably go totally bonkers. Enjoy the sailing."

Derek took another step up the stairs before he turned around again. He was safe. The kids were entirely spellbound.

"You mean you've had another vision?" Mackie asked.

"Didn't Kit tell you?"

"I didn't know what the new one was about," Kit explained. "I was too afraid to ask."

"Well, maybe it won't seem so bad to you as it did to me," Derek said. He grabbed a chair by the wall and pulled it up to the table. "In my latest vision, I actually went into the house," he said as he sat down. "Don't ask me how I got there but I did. I remember going down to the cellar. It was awful. Are you sure you guys can take it? Do you want me to go on?"

The four kids nodded emphatically.

"I saw the grave," Derek said. "There was a little cross and the captain's name was on it. All I remember after that is running from the house as fast as my legs could carry me. When I got to the road, I turned around. That was the worst part. I saw her."

"Evangeline?" Phoebe asked.

Derek nodded solemnly.

"You saw her with your own eyes?" Pink asked. "That's even worse than the dream you told me about the other day."

Derek nodded. "I thought that was a dream. Maybe it was really my first vision."

"But you're the guy who doesn't believe in ghosts," Mackie said. "Why would she pick on you of all people?"

"Because I was a nonbeliever," Derek said. "Later on, when we got to talking, she explained she likes to turn nonbelievers into believers. She's says that's a usual thing with ghosts."

"You *talked* with her?" Kit asked.

"That's when I had to make my complete turnabout in the belief department," Derek said. "First she was beckoning to me. She was standing on her widow's walk and reaching out for me. I was paralyzed with horror. I couldn't take a step in any direction. She started talking to me. I said she couldn't be real and she said she was going to haunt me whether I liked it or not. We started to talk, but I got so frightened I woke up then and there. Otherwise I probably would have had a heart attack in my sleep."

When he finished, Derek had to keep his lips very stiff. If he hadn't, they would have formed the biggest smile. Phoebe and Mackie and Pink and Kit were all ears now. There was worry and even a trace of fear on their faces.

"Tonight I'm going back to the mansion," Derek announced. "I have to see it again."

"You're going to the cellar?" Pink asked.

"Even if I have to break in," Derek said. "But if I see there is no grave there, I'll know once and for all that my vision was just a dumb dream. It's the only way I'll ever get some quality sleep, alas." Derek had never used the word *alas* before, but he felt it added a nice dramatic touch.

"But plenty of people swear there's no grave there," Pink said. "There's just a hollow where a root cellar could have been."

"I'll have to see for myself," Derek said. "Tonight."

"You're going alone?" Mackie asked.

"What kind of person would go with me?" Derek asked.

"A decent person," Mackie said.

"A brave person," Phoebe said.

"A loyal friend," Pink said.

"A caring sister," Kit said.

"You guys would go with me?" Derek gasped.

"There's no way you're going without us," Pink said.

"You mean it?" Derek asked.

The four kids nodded, and Derek made a little bow of thanks. "We'll meet on Dune Road at midnight."

"We can't go now?" Pink asked.

"If someone sees us sneaking into the Coffin mansion in broad daylight, we'll be arrested," Derek said. "We've got to be careful or we could end up in the slammer."

"I'll set my alarm for quarter to twelve," Phoebe said.

"Me too," said Mackie. "I'll sneak out of my house and I'll meet you guys on Dune Road."

"I don't know how I'll stand the tension till then," Kit said.

"Why not let Pink take you guys sailing," Derek suggested. "Your offer still stand?"

"You bet," Pink said. "Why not come along, Derek?"

"It's better for me to be by myself for a while," Derek said. "I'll probably meditate or something."

"Till midnight then," Phoebe said.

"On Dune Road," Mackie said.

"Everyone bring flashlights," Pink said.

The four kids stood and filed out of the kitchen. Derek waved to them as they crossed the lawn and started down toward Dock Street. He looked at the clock above the stove. It was four. If he hurried, he'd have just enough time to visit the mansion and get things ready for tonight. It would be a crime to invite four people out in the middle of the night and not give them something for their efforts.

9

IT WAS ALMOST SUPPERTIME when Derek got back to his grandmother's house. His visit to the Coffin mansion had been trickier than he had imagined. Derek tried to take it philosophically. Breaking in a new assistant could be a chore for anyone.

"Supper's almost ready," Herb said as Derek let the screen door slam behind him. "Five minutes, Edna!" he hollered. "Five minutes, Kit and Margo!"

"Margo can't hear you," Derek said. "She's in the barn putting away her bike."

"Little late in the day for bike riding," Herb said.

Derek decided to ignore Herb's comment. He was in no position to tell Herb or anyone else that he had been riding with Margo.

Herb pulled five baked potatoes from the oven and set them on the counter to cool. On the top of the stove was a kettle of fish stew. Herb had gotten the recipe from Pink's mother, and it was now the favorite meal in two Plymouth Island households.

"How's it going?" Derek asked as he sat down at the table.

"At the theater, you mean?" Herb asked.

"Just because I'm not working there doesn't mean I'm not interested."

"It's okay," Herb said. "Quieter without you. Got to admit that."

"Does that mean I'm missed?"

"I sure hope we can put you back on the payroll soon," Herb said. "How's your life these days?"

"Moving along," Derek said noncommittally. He didn't want Herb to think he was doing badly, but he didn't want Herb to think he was doing all that great either. "I got some ideas," he said. "I'm working on something."

"Profit-making?"

"Could be," Derek said. "If I play my cards right."

"Well, if business picks up at the theater, I hope you'll be free to come back."

"Don't worry, Herb," said Derek. "It'll be over and done with soon enough."

"One of your get-rich-quick schemes?"

"I figure if you're going to get rich, why waste time?"

Herb laughed and started dishing out the stew into bowls. "Supper's on!" he shouted.

Grandma appeared from the front of the house and Kit ran down the back stairs. The screen door slammed and Margo came in. Herb set out the bowls on the table for them.

Derek was enjoying his meal, looking forward to the night that lay before him. He would have liked to dawdle over supper for once, but Herb and his grandmother were wolfing down their food in a way that Derek thought was physically impossible for anyone over sixteen.

"Where's the fire?" he asked.

"We've got a dress rehearsal before the show," his grandmother said.

"On a Tuesday night?" Kit asked.

"Our ingenue twisted her ankle water-skiing," Herb said. "We have to run her understudy through the part."

Grandma Edna took her bowl and Herb's to the sink. Herb grabbed a hunk of bread before he and Grandma headed across the parking lot to the theater.

"I thought kids were supposed to leave the table first," Margo said. "Shouldn't they have asked for permission?"

"It's different if you're going to work," Derek said.

"That makes sense to me," Margo said. She stuck her spoon in her mouth and played with it thoughtfully. "How are the visions coming, Derek?"

"You know about them?" Kit asked.

"Oh, sure," Margo said. "Derek told me and I've been telling everyone in town."

"But they're private," Kit said.

"But Derek told me to . . ."

Derek interrupted her. If he hadn't, she could have ruined everything. "It doesn't matter," he said. "My life's an open book anyway. I have nothing to hide."

"But I thought you . . ."

"Please, Margo," Derek said. "It doesn't matter who knows about my visions."

"They're not visions," Kit said. "Don't let them frighten you, Margo."

How Kit got the impression that Margo

was frightened was beyond Derek. Margo looked about as scared as a kid in a candy store. As a matter of fact, she seemed to be enjoying the spot Derek was in.

"We're taking Derek over to the Coffin mansion tonight just to prove there's nothing to his visions," Kit said. "You want to come?"

"More than anything!" Margo squealed.

"It might be a little terrifying for you," Kit cautioned.

"But I love being terrified," Margo said. "Except by thunder and lightning."

Derek nodded but he prayed that Kit hadn't noticed the enormous wink Margo was giving him. Subtlety wasn't Margo's strong suit. What bothered Derek more, however, was that he needed her more than she needed him. And what bothered him the most was that by now she knew it.

DEREK DIDN'T DARE lie down on his bed that night for fear that he just might fall asleep. Instead, he sat by the window and watched the crowds leave the Red Barn after the show. He listened to Grandma say good night to Herb and lock up the house before she went to bed.

Then he pulled a flashlight from the top drawer of his bureau and left the room. Kit was waiting for him in the kitchen and Margo was with her. The only light came from the refrigerator, where Kit was rooting about for leftovers.

"How can anyone eat at a time like this?" he whispered.

"Margo says she needs her strength," Kit whispered back. She held out a piece of Cheddar cheese to her sister.

Margo took the cheese. "Can't work on an empty stomach, I always say." Derek gave her the dirtiest look he could muster. "I mean, I can't go out at night hungry, if you know what I mean," she corrected herself.

They closed the kitchen door as quietly as possible and headed for the garage. Then they walked their bikes down the driveway and got on them as soon as they reached Water Street. Kit led the way again, pedaling furiously toward Dune Road. They slowed down. The others were meeting them there, but they hadn't bothered to decide at which point.

Off to the right, beyond the houses with their well-kept lawns and ten-foot-high privet hedges, Derek spotted a glow. Kit must have noticed it too. He heard her brakes squeak.

"How late are we?" Kit asked.

"You're five minutes early," Pink said. "We just happened to be ten minutes early."

"Who's going to lead?" Phoebe asked. "And who's going to take up the rear? I'm too scared to do either. I want to be in the middle."

"I'll lead," Kit said. "Margo, you stay close behind me."

"I'll take the rear," Mackie said.

The six of them got on their bikes and made their way Indian file down Dune Road. The closer they got to the Coffin mansion, the slower they pedaled. A hundred feet from the house, the kids got off their bikes. Without a word, they walked slowly toward the shabby picket fence in front of Widow Coffin's house.

"Let's walk around to the back," Kit said. "That's where we saw the light."

"I'm too frightened," Margo said anxiously. "I guess I don't like being scared. I'll stay here and wait for you guys."

"You sure?" Phoebe asked. "Would you like one of us to stay with you."

"Oh, no!" Margo said adamantly. "I'm okay on my own. You don't have to treat me like a little girl."

Derek sighed. Margo was carrying off her part as though she had been born to it. He even felt more relaxed that she would find the sheet inside where he had left it for her. Then he followed the other kids around to the back of the house. Out of the corner of his eye, he saw Margo dashing up the front steps and into the house.

"It's gone," Kit said almost joyously. She was pointing to the window on the second floor. "There's no light now. There's nothing to worry about."

"But the grave," Phoebe said. "Someone's got to see if the grave is in the cellar. That's what we're here for."

"What do you mean 'someone's' got to look?" Mackie asked. "We're all going inside."

"I'm too frightened," Phoebe said. "I'll stay here and wait. I'll go back and keep Margo company."

"You can't," Derek said sternly.

"What's it matter?" she asked.

Derek thought quickly. "We need as many witnesses as possible," he said.

"If we all go, we'll be okay," Pink said.

He took a step toward the back door on the porch, and the others followed. He reached for Derek's flashlight and aimed it at the door.

When he shook the handle, the door swung open, creaking loudly on its hinges. The kids stood back before they followed Pink inside.

Once, perhaps, the room had been a kitchen, but there was no sign of it now. Pink pointed the flashlight around the room. The light lingered on a door, the one that led down to the cellar. Derek wanted to tell Pink that he'd hit the right door, but he couldn't. He had to wait until Pink opened the door, peered down the steps, and motioned for the others to follow.

With each step, the stairs groaned. One step behind Pink was Kit, then Mackie, then Phoebe, with Derek at the tail end. One step, two steps, three steps. The groans grew louder. Four steps, five steps, six steps. The cold, clammy air of the basement sent a chill through Derek. He could only imagine—and hope—how much worse it must be for the others.

Seven steps, eight steps, nine steps. Pink stopped. He had come to the basement floor. The others still on the stairs stood still as Pink flashed his light, first at the cobwebs that dangled from the beams, then at the blackened walls. The flashlight found the floor and moved about it slowly, methodically.

The light flickered and came to a rest. There it was! The white stick rising from the

dirt floor was no more than five feet high. The stick across it was almost as long. Pink's flashlight stuck to the lettering on it:

CAPTAIN RALPH COFFIN, 1801–1871

Just under it was his epitaph:

GOOD RIDDANCE TO BAD RUBBISH——EVANGELINE

Widows and Witches hadn't mentioned the captain's first name, and Derek had had to improvise for that and an epitaph.

There was a collective gasp from the children. Derek joined in to keep them company.

"It's the grave," Kit moaned. "It's just what was in your vision, Derek. It wasn't a nightmare. It was absolutely true!"

Before she had finished speaking, all five children were racing up the stairs and through the house and down the back steps. As they flew through the grass, Derek grabbed Phoebe's and Kit's hands and came to a dead stop, causing them to stop in their tracks too.

"Let go of me, Derek Malloy!" Phoebe shrieked.

"We're scared! Please, Derek!" Kit shouted.

"But look," Derek pleaded. "Look back at the house!"

"I don't see anything," Mackie said.

"Haven't we already seen too much?" Pink asked.

"Flash the light at the roof," Derek commanded. "At the widow's walk."

"You're crazy, Derek," Pink said.

"Please, Pink," Derek pleaded, hoping he wasn't pushing too far.

Pink aimed the flashlight at the second story.

"Higher," Derek said. "At the widow's walk."

"Oh, no," Phoebe moaned.

"It can't be," Mackie said. "No way!"

"Are we all hallucinating?" Kit asked. "Are we all as crazy as Derek?"

There she was. A tiny figure, cloaked in white, stood at the railing. She flapped her arms crazily and then she began to dance about like a maniac. Then she danced and flapped at the same time.

"She's beckoning," Derek said.

"Not to me," Kit said.

"Me either," Phoebe shrieked. "I'm too young to die."

The kids started to run again. It was Derek's cue. He fell to the ground and grabbed for his foot with both hands. "Ooooooh! Aaaaaaaa! Oooooooh!" he wailed. "I tripped on a rock. I've broken something."

Phoebe, Mackie, Kit, and Pink came back and hovered around him. It took them almost five minutes to get him back on his feet and reassure him that nothing was broken. That was just enough time for Margo to get herself out of the house, Derek figured.

Soon they were all pedaling back home. Derek's feet pedaled fast too, but the rest of him was relaxed. All things considered, the evening had gone remarkably well, so well in fact that he was considering giving Margo a significant bonus. With the money he planned to make off Evangeline, he had a feeling he could afford to be generous.

10

DEREK WOKE UP the next morning to the sound of someone knocking at his door. His elation from the night before evaporated as soon as he saw Margo's scowling face.

"How come you couldn't give me a day job?" she asked. "Isn't there a law against making eight-year-olds work at night?"

"You going to report me to the child welfare authorities?" Derek asked.

"Maybe I'll tell Grandma," she said as she sat down on the foot of his bed.

"Tell Grandma and the whole deal is off," he said.

"Maybe I won't tell Grandma," Margo said thoughtfully. "If you give me a raise, that is."

"But you've only been working a couple of hours," Derek protested. "You can't ask for a raise yet."

"Give me an extra two bucks and I'll keep my mouth shut," Margo said.

Derek resented Margo for pushing him into giving her a raise even though he had already decided to give her a bonus. "I'll give it to you at the end of the week."

"In advance," Margo said.

"But I won't be getting my loot till then."

"Now."

Reluctantly Derek pulled two one-dollar bills from the wallet on his bed table and gave them to her. "Don't worry," he said. "They're unmarked."

"I love you," Margo said after she had counted the bills. Then she skipped out of the room.

When Derek got downstairs, Kit was still sitting at the kitchen table. From the two cups, two plates, and two glasses on the counter, he could tell that Grandma and Herb had already eaten their breakfast.

"How's it going?" he asked as he poured himself some juice and popped two slices of whole-wheat bread into the toaster.

"I was kind of hoping you'd tell me that

everything about last night was a dream," Kit said.

"It happened, Kit," he said somberly. "Whether we like it or not."

"There really was a grave in the cellar? And that thing on the widow's walk was the ghost of Evangeline Coffin?"

"Would you like me to say it was all a figment of your imagination?"

"I don't want to believe in visions and ghosts," Kit insisted.

"But the only alternative is that we're crazy," he said. "You'd prefer to be out of your mind?"

Kit dropped a crust on her plate. "Rather be crazy?" she asked, more to herself than Derek. "Maybe I would. I know I'm afraid to ask how you slept."

"Not very well, I'm afraid."

"Please, Derek. Tell me you slept like a log."

"If only that were true."

"You toss and turn?"

"Worse than that."

"Another vision?"

Derek nodded, and Kit put her hands to her ears as if to shield herself from his words.

"I don't want to know about it," she said.

"I won't burden you," he said. "We all saw what we saw but the visions are mine."

"We'll have another meeting," Kit said. "This afternoon. You and me and Phoebe and Pink and Mackie. Tell us when we're all together."

"But you don't really want to know about my latest vision."

"Just because I don't want to know doesn't mean I'm not going to find out," she said. "You're my brother. It's my job to help out when I can."

Derek was touched, but he also felt uncomfortable. Was that a twinge of guilt he was feeling for fooling his sister? He knew he could still call off the project, but he also knew he wouldn't, not when he was only hours away from pulling off his greatest scheme ever.

"WE'RE READY to hear the vision," Kit said. "Are you ready to tell us?"

Derek looked around at his sister and Pink and Mackie and Phoebe. They were sitting in a circle on the beach where they had had their clambake only the week before. There were other spots they could have picked for their meeting, but the beach was the most private of all.

100

"I'm ready," Derek said. "But it's not easy. She came to me again."

"Evangeline?" Phoebe asked.

Derek nodded as sadly as he could and shrugged.

"Was she wearing the same getup?"

"What do you mean 'getup'?"

"Well, it looked like one of those cheap, no-iron sheets," Phoebe said.

Derek tried not to show how offended he was by her remark. That sheet had cost almost seven dollars. How dare Phoebe Wilson call it cheap? "It's what Evangeline wears all the time," he said. "I don't know where she got it or how much she paid."

Phoebe cocked one eyebrow. Evidently, she thought ghosts had the same problems with clothes that regular human beings did. Derek didn't know how to convince her otherwise. Nor did he have the time to try.

"She talked to me this time," he said. "We had a regular conversation. She's got a problem and wants me to solve it for her."

"Why you?" Kit asked.

"I'm the only human being she's been able to get through to recently."

"Does Evangeline think you're on a higher spiritual plane than the rest of us?" Mackie asked. "That's very significant, I hear, in the spiritual world."

"We didn't get into that sort of stuff," Derek admitted. "She wanted to get right to the problem."

"What's that?" Mackie asked.

"She knows I'm good with money and she needs some," Derek said.

Derek saw the other kids draw back.

"What on earth does a ghost need money for?" Phoebe asked. "They don't pay rent or buy food. And that thing Evangeline was wearing last night, whatever it was, had to be a hand-me-down."

"She needs the money to pay her ransom so she can go free at last," Derek said.

"That makes no sense at all," Pink said suspiciously.

"But it's very plausible," Derek insisted. "It's just like you said, Pink. Evangeline's ghost is being held prisoner in the Coffin mansion. It's her punishment for murdering her husband. She's been there almost a century, and the spirit world won't let her go until some money is left at her husband's grave."

"I don't believe it," Kit said. "Are you up to something, Derek?"

"Did you see the light in the window?" Derek asked.

Kit nodded slowly, but not happily.

"Didn't you all see the grave in the basement?"

All of them nodded now, equally slowly.

"And the ghost on the widow's walk? What about her?"

"She was for real," Phoebe said. "I saw her."

"So did I," Derek said. "I heard her too. Now she wants money and if she doesn't get some right away, she's going to haunt everyone on this island the way she's haunting me."

"Everyone?" Mackie asked.

"The four of you especially," Derek said. "You're the guys who've seen her. Remember, I didn't ask you to come with me to the Coffin mansion. I didn't ask you to get involved in my visions. You guys insisted."

"How much money, Derek?" Pink asked.

"She didn't name a specific amount," Derek said. " 'Something suitable' was all she said."

"And then the spirit world will let her go?" Kit asked.

"That's what she says," Derek replied.

"Sounds weird to me," Pink said. "I don't

want to believe any of it. I don't know why the spirit world would need money, but I know I'm not crazy. I saw what I saw. I say we give Evangeline a hand. Got any ideas as to how we get the money, Derek?"

"All Derek ever thinks about is how to get money," Kit said. "That's why Evangeline went to him."

"That's very sweet of you to say," Derek said. "But Evangeline has already given the matter some consideration. She says we should have a house tour. She thinks lots of people would pay good money for a tour of a historic house, especially one that's haunted."

"Will she make an appearance?" Phoebe asked.

"She promises it will be her farewell appearance," Derek said. "But not if there are any doubters around. Evangeline says she can't handle an identity crisis now."

"But how can we screen out the doubters?" Kit asked.

"Evangeline says kids only," Derek added.

"But kids can't pay much for a house tour," Phoebe said.

"Evangeline says it's the thought that counts in the spiritual world," Derek said. "She wants the tour to take place the day after to-morrow."

"Friday?" Mackie asked.

"Friday the thirteenth," Derek said as he looked knowingly at the others. When they looked back at him just as knowingly, Derek knew he had it made. He'd lost a lot of sleep over this scheme, but somehow he knew he could muster enough energy to see it through. By Saturday the fourteenth, he hoped to have just enough strength left to count his money.

11

FRIDAYS THE THIRTEENTH were supposed to be gloomy, maybe even scary, and so when Derek Malloy woke up that morning and looked out his window, he was delighted. While everyone else was sorry that the clouds and the wind would keep them from the beach, Derek figured the weather that day was just right for what he had in mind.

But there were many things to do that day, and Derek didn't have too much free time to congratulate himself on the weather. While Kit and Mackie and Pink and Phoebe were taking care of informing every child they could about the house tour that evening, Derek had to check out the mansion once more and rehearse his younger sister.

It wasn't until late that afternoon that Derek had finished his chores. He could only hope that the others had held up their end as well. He ate dinner with the rest of the family and even volunteered to clean up afterward. It wasn't like him, but it got Grandma Edna and Herb off to the Red Barn a little earlier than usual. That gave Margo more time to get over to the mansion.

At seven-thirty, just as the sun was setting, Derek and Kit got on their bikes. Clouds still covered the sky and it was beginning to rain. The wind still blew in long gusts. Derek worried that a storm might scare away some of the kids. He was glad that Margo had gone on ahead an hour before.

He stopped brooding, however, as soon as he and Kit turned the last corner on Dune Road and the Coffin mansion came into view. Standing outside the picket fence were almost fifty kids, all waiting to help free Evangeline from her ghostly prison and perhaps get a good scare in the bargain.

"Okay, kids," Derek called as he led Kit through the crowd. "Make way. The tour will start in five minutes. Don't forget to have your money ready."

He led Kit up the front steps where Mackie and Pink and Phoebe were waiting. "You guys, wait here," he said. He leaned against the front door and shoved. The door opened.

In the front hall, Derek lit a kerosene lamp with a kitchen match. The lamp and the matches were part of the equipment he had brought over that afternoon. He set the lamp in a corner and stood at the center of the room. He waved his arms in the air and noticed his shadow doing likewise on the opposite wall. He liked the effect. Maybe it would scare some of the younger kids.

"Ready in here," Derek shouted. "Bring on the kids."

Derek stood back as Kit and Phoebe led the children up the front steps and into the house. Pink and Mackie were bringing up the rear. Most of them were already wide-eyed, even frightened looking. They were looking for something to terrify them, and Derek wasn't about to let them down.

"Okay, kids," he said. "Welcome to the Coffin mansion. Shut up and I'll begin the tour. This is probably the first and last tour, so listen closely. We're in the living room now. For poor Captain Ralph Coffin, his living room was also his dying room. It's where Evangeline strangled him to death with her bare hands in a fit of jealous pique. You can see the bloodstains on the floor."

Derek pointed to a brownish smudge he had discovered that afternoon. In the daylight, it hadn't looked at all like a bloodstain. Derek figured it would by night.

There was a startled gasp from the kids.

"How come there's blood?" Pink asked from the back. "People don't bleed when you strangle them."

"Immediately after strangling the captain, Evangeline shot him through the heart," Derek said.

"What a horrid lady," a little girl whispered.

"But a thorough one," Derek assured his audience. "Shall we head downstairs? We'll be following the path by which Evangeline dragged the captain's poor lifeless body. Step right this way, kids."

Derek picked up the kerosene lamp and led the way to the back of the house. He opened the door to the cellar and started down the stairs. When he was standing over the cross, he turned around and watched as fifty pairs of small feet walked down the creeking steps.

"Here it is, kids," Derek said when everyone was downstairs. He raised the lamp to give the kids a better glimpse of the cobwebs as well as the burial marker. "Here's where she brought the captain for his final resting place."

"It's a tacky cross," a little boy said.

"Under the circumstances, it was a very thoughtful gesture," Derek said. He stood back and let the kids look around on their own. Most of them were too afraid to take more than two or three steps toward the grave.

"As some of you may already know," Derek continued, "Evangeline has been haunting me lately, and if we don't leave her some cash now, she's going to haunt you too. Get your change ready."

Derek picked up a large canvas bag that he had left in the cellar that afternoon. He set it before the grave and dropped half a dozen of his own quarters into it. That was to show the kids that he believed everything he said. "Evangeline told me yesterday that if there's enough money in the bag, she'll thank you all personally later on."

The roar that went up at that moment was greater than anything Derek could have anticipated. In no time at all, the kids were shoving their fists into their pockets for all the change they had. They were stepping toward the sack and dumping their money into it. The ping!—ping!—ping! of quarters and dimes and nickels and pennies mingling was hypnotic for Derek.

"Anyone want to see the rest of the house?" he asked as he tightened the cord at the neck of the sack and pulled it up over his shoulder.

"Will we see Evangeline?" one of the little boys asked.

"I'd say you have a ghost of a chance," Derek said as ominously as he could.

He started up the stairs, and the boys and girls followed. Derek looked back to make sure everyone was with him. He noticed Pink kneeling at the grave and investigating. "You coming, Pink?" he called.

"I'll explore a bit," Pink said. "I'll catch up in a minute."

Derek didn't like Pink lingering in the cellar, but he couldn't dawdle now. He had collected his haul, and, like the actors at Grandma Edna's theater, he still had to give the rest of his performance.

He climbed the steps to the first floor and

led the kids down the center hall. Then he led them up the next flight of stairs to the second floor.

"You're moving too fast," Kit yelled. "Slow down. Tell the kids about the second floor."

"Nothing ever happened on the second floor," Derek said.

Kit paused before one door. "That's the room the light was coming from," she said. "Are you sure there wasn't even a minor poisoning in here?"

"Please, Kit," Derek said. "It's no time to be glib. This mansion is seriously haunted. I'll show you when we get to the widow's walk." Derek headed toward the last flight of stairs.

"I'm going to hang behind anyway," Phoebe said.

"Too afraid to go on the widow's walk?" Derek asked.

"Too interested in looking around down here," she said. "Kit and Mackie can help you with the kids. I'll catch up."

Derek didn't like the tone of what Phoebe had said. But he had no choice now but to move onward and upward. He climbed the last flight of steps, listening to the patter of a hundred little feet behind him. He looked back. Thank heavens that Kit and Mackie were still guiding the kids.

When Derek got to the top step, he leaned hard against the door to the roof and shoved. The door gave, and a blast of cold air struck him in the face. A storm was coming for sure. The rain was getting heavier, and in the distance he detected a small bolt of lightning flash across the twilight horizon.

"Evangeline?" he whispered in his loudest stage whisper. "Are you there?"

At the sound of Derek's voice, a small, ethereal figure swathed in white turned toward the crowd. She stood on the widow's walk and her hands gripped the railing. "Ooooh, ooooh, ooooh," she wailed. "Derek, is that you?"

"It's me, Evangeline," Derek said. "And I've brought the kids with me."

Derek turned from Evangeline to the kids. Fifty pairs of eyes were so wide open that he could hardly believe they would ever shut again. Each child stood paralyzed with fear and excitement. Derek suspected that none of them was even breathing.

"Did you bring money?" Evangeline wailed in a squeaky, high-pitched voice.

"I got it right here," Derek said, "in this sack."

"Then dump the sack right here," Evangeline wailed. "Oooh, oooh, oooh, Derek."

"Wouldn't you like me to hold onto it for you?" he asked.

"Dump it on the floor," Evangeline squeaked. "Pronto."

Derek didn't like letting go of the sack, but he wasn't about to get into an argument. He set the sack at Evangeline's feet.

"How come she's so short?" Kit asked.

Derek tried not to react to the suspicion in her voice. "Please, Kit," he whispered. "She's very touchy about her height. The reason she killed her husband was because he was dating a taller woman."

As Derek checked out the crowd, he could see that the kids were looking a lot less frightened now. Kit and Mackie were even beginning to look downright suspicious.

"It's raining," Derek said quickly. "It's time to get going. Everyone downstairs!"

"Bye, bye, children," the ghost squeaked. "Thanks for the ransom. Oooh, oooh, oooh!"

"Bye, Evangeline," Derek said.

As he started to shepherd the children back toward the stairs, Pink and Phoebe rushed into the room. Pink was holding the grave marker and Phoebe was holding the battery-run lamp that he had left in the back bedroom. As soon as he saw it, Derek promised himself that he would never leave any bedroom, even his own, undone again.

"We smell a rat," Pink yelled.

"A rat named Derek Malloy," Phoebe shouted.

"The paint can't be more than a week old on this marker," Pink said. "You got these sticks from the boatyard, didn't you?"

"And I saw you buy this lamp at the bookstore," Phoebe said.

"I remember," Mackie exclaimed. "I was there too."

"That's the light from the window?" Kit asked incredulously. "Derek, how could you?"

Before Derek could brace himself for any kind of defense, a huge bolt of lightning illuminated the sky. A second later, thunder enveloped the house in a blast that took away even Derek's breath.

"Aaaaah, aaaaah, aaaaaah!" Evangeline screamed at the top of her lungs in a voice that was very different from the one she had had before. "Someone get me out of here! Quick! Before I die!"

Kit walked over to the ghost. "Before you die?" she asked as the rain fell harder. "Didn't anyone ever tell you you're already dead, Evangeline, dear?" Kit pulled the white sheet that covered all of Evangeline's body. There stood Margo, a very terrified Margo.

"Margo!" Kit yelled. "How could you get yourself involved in another one of Derek's schemes?"

"You tell and you're fired," Derek cautioned.

"I quit, Derek!" she sobbed. "I'm never working for you again. The hours stink and the pay's rotten. Most of all, I hate the clothes. It's not even real clothes. It's a stupid sheet, for crying out loud," Margo added, crying out loud as she said it.

The lightning flashed and the thunder rolled again. Soon Margo wasn't the only little kid who was screaming. The younger kids were beginning to fret and the older ones were looking downright angry. Derek's audience was turning into a mob, a very unhappy mob. Derek didn't have to think twice to know that it was time to make his exit.

He saw the sack of money lying at Margo's feet. He wanted to grab it, but Pink was across

the room and clutching it tightly before Derek could move toward it.

Derek turned on his heels and flew through the crowd at the top of the stairs. He raced down to the landing, ran along the hall, and turned down the last flight of stairs. Behind him he could hear hundreds of feet clamoring after him. Some of the kids were yelling, "Get him! Get him!" He heard a voice that he recognized as Kit's screaming, "Don't let the rat get away!"

Derek didn't turn to see if they were catching up with him. He ran all the faster across the downstairs hall and tore out onto the porch.

It wasn't until he hit the bottom step that he came to a halt. Car after car was pulling up in front of the house, and parents, dozens of them, were stalking through the rain and up the front walk.

As the parents drew closer, Derek could see that they looked mad too. It wouldn't be more than a few minutes before he would be trapped between two angry mobs, both out to get him.

Could he get away? Could he snake through the mobs before he was caught? Was there time? Did he have any strength left?

Derek took the deepest breath he had ever

taken. It was a do-or-die situation and the odds were stacked mightily against him. He took another, even deeper breath. It was the breath that cost him his last chance at a getaway. Just as he was exhaling, he could feel hands grabbing his wrists. Two of the hands belonged to Mackie. The other two belonged to Pink. They had him. It was over.

12

"**D**EREK? You up there?"

He heard her voice and clenched his arms more tightly around the branch of the old elm tree.

"Come on down, dear. I know you're there."

"How can you tell for sure?" he whispered hoarsely.

"I see your left leg dangling from the branch," his grandmother said. "Unless it's been severed from your hip, the rest of you should be nearby."

He hugged the branch tighter. "I'm never coming down," he moaned. "I'm too ashamed."

"Ashamed of what you did?" his grandmother asked. "Or ashamed of getting caught?"

"A lot of both, I guess," he said. "I'm too ashamed to tell you anything else."

His grandmother flashed a flashlight in his eyes. "The storm's over, dear. It's time we cleared up the debris."

"The kids have their money back," Derek said. "Pink and Mackie took care of that. And the parents got the kids back. How was I to know they'd get suspicious and form a posse to come after me? If there's any debris, I'm it."

"You still have some apologies to make, to the kids and to their parents. You might also think about some amends to your sisters and your friends. You led them on quite a merry chase, Derek."

"Haven't I suffered enough?" he pleaded. "Wasn't getting stuck between two mobs more than enough punishment? I thought I'd die of humiliation when you and Herb pulled up to take me prisoner. What more is there?"

"Oh, I believe you're right," his grandmother said. "As long as you promise to take care of the apologies and the amends. What matters now is getting you back on the straight and narrow. Are you ready for that?"

"I feel I'm still out on a limb, Grandma," he said.

He heard his grandmother laugh. "That's because you still are," she said. "Come down this minute."

Derek grabbed the trunk of the tree and pulled himself around it. Slowly he let himself slither down to the ground. "Tomorrow I'll apologize to everyone," Derek said. "Do you think they'll forgive me for conning them?"

"I think they had too much fun with your stunt to hold a grudge for long," his grandmother said. "But that doesn't make it right. Remember that, dear."

"Do you forgive me?"

"I forgive you."

"It's not just because you're my grandmother and that's what grandmothers are supposed to do, is it?"

"Partly so, I suspect," Grandma Edna said. "Partly because after Margo quieted down, she said it was the best time she's ever had and no one ever took such great care of her as you did. You get a couple points there, Derek. I gather you even pay a pretty fair wage."

"Will you ever let me work in the theater again?"

"Herb and I have discussed that already,"

Grandma Edna said. "Can you start tomorrow morning?"

"Really? You mean it?"

"We figure it's our contribution to the rehabilitation of the youth of America," his grandmother sighed. "At least till the end of the summer. And after what we've seen tonight, the theater is where you belong."

As Derek moved toward the house, he felt his grandmother's arm around his shoulder.

"I think so too," Derek said. "It's just exactly where I belong."

"You're just on the wrong side of the footlights," Grandma Edna said. "You're a ham, Derek. You belong on the stage."

Maybe his grandmother was right, Derek thought. He promised himself that he would give that some consideration. As he walked up the kitchen steps, he also promised himself that he was going to stay as far away as he could from any more of his brilliant ideas for the rest of August.

September, he had a feeling, was bound to be another story.